SMASH!

Exploring the Mysteries
of the Universe with the
Large Hadron Collider

They say an author's books are like her children, and so I dedicate this
baby to my husband, Tony Liss, who made it possible. (Alison, Caitlin,
and Eli, you're still my favorites!) —S.L.

For Sid and Lena—two charmed quarks —J.W.

Graphic Universe™
A division of Lerner Publishing Group, Inc.
241 First Avenue North
Minneapolis, MN 55401 USA

For reading levels and more information, look up this title at www.lernerbooks.com.

The illustrator has used images from the CERN press office as the basis for some of the artwork for this book.

Main body text set in CCMildMannered 7/8.4.
Typeface provided by Comicraft.

Library of Congress Cataloging-in-Publication Data

Names: Latta, Sara L., author. | Weigel, Jeff, 1958– illustrator.
Title: Smash! : exploring the mysteries of the universe with the Large Hadron Collider / written by Sara Latta ;
    illustrated by Jeff Weigel.
Other titles: Exploring the mysteries of the universe with the Large Hadron Collider
Description: Minneapolis, MN : Graphic Universe, a division of Lerner Publishing Group, Inc., [2017] | Includes
    bibliographical references. | Audience: 13–18. | Audience: 9 to 12.
Identifiers: LCCN 2016017321 (print) | LCCN 2016021130 (ebook) | ISBN 9781467785518 (lb ; alk. paper) |
    ISBN 9781512430707 (pb ; alk. paper) | ISBN 9781512427011 (eb pdf)
Subjects: LCSH: Large Hadron Collider (France and Switzerland)—Juvenile literature. | Higgs bosons—Juvenile
    literature. | Particles (Nuclear physics)—Juvenile literature. | European Organization for Nuclear Research—
    Juvenile literature.
Classification: LCC QC787.P73 L38 2017 (print) | LCC QC787.P73 (ebook) | DDC 539.7/36—dc23

LC record available at https://lccn.loc.gov/2016017321

Manufactured in the United States of America
1-37905-19175-7/19/2016

SMASH!

Sara Latta

illustrated by Jeff Weigel

Graphic Universe™ • Minneapolis

Foreword

When I was very little, I spent a lot of time pondering the universe and wondering if it could end—and what that could possibly even mean! I also wondered a lot about "empty" space. I felt certain that if I could take away everything from the space in front of me, including light, what would be left could not be *nothing* . . . but I had no idea what it *could* be. By a very circuitous route, I discovered that physicists are the people who try to answer these questions. This led me to embark on my own study of physics, where I eventually learned to make and use devices for particle accelerators that could detect what actually exists in what we physicists call the "vacuum of space-time."

I am now a professor of physics, and I've spent about thirty-five years searching for and studying fundamental particles with teams of exceptional physicists, engineers, students and technicians on a number of great experiments. We've made some magnificent discoveries, all of which are included in *Smash!*.

There is no doubt now that the vacuum of space-time is not empty. It is filled with the Higgs field, verified by the discovery of the Higgs boson. (You'll learn more about all of this in the pages that follow.) On July 4, 2012, Fabiola Gianotti and I—the leaders of the CERN facility's ATLAS and CMS experiments at the time—announced this discovery. Though a confirmation of the Higgs boson completes a theory of nature at its most fundamental level, it is not the end of the story by any means. This theory, the Standard Model, only represents what we understand—and that is less than 5 percent of the universe.

Sara Latta and Jeff Weigel's graphic novel gives a nicely illustrated and humorous view of the study of particle physics at CERN, the laboratory where the Higgs was discovered. Latta does a marvelous job of encapsulating the incredible history of physical thought, from the pre-Socratic Greek philosophers to modern-day particle physicists at the Large Hadron Collider. It's very accessible, entertaining, and thorough. It covers pretty much everything we know!

Smash! presents all of the fundamental particles and forces, which I like to call "the genetic code of our universe," to the non-expert in a way that may be the best I have seen to date. Weigel's illustrations depict the interactions of quarks, leptons, and force-carrying bosons in a way that's easy to remember. And then, like a Hollywood teaser for a sequel, the graphic novel ends with a glimpse of our current focus on what lies beyond the Standard Model, in the dark side of the universe. I don't think very many people know we've entered these completely uncharted new territories.

Smash! does a great job of showing how the discovery of the Higgs boson marks the end of one era and the beginning of a new one. I believe that *Smash!* will inspire kids who ponder the universe and its vast emptiness, like I did years ago, to join us in this millennia-old quest to understand where we are and how it all works.

Joe Incandela
Yzurdiaga Chair in Experimental Science and Distinguished Professor of Physics
University of California Santa Barbara
Member, National Academy of Sciences

"The most beautiful experience we can have is the mysterious. It is the fundamental emotion which stands at the cradle of true art and true science."

Albert Einstein, 1930

NICK! YO, NICK! OVER HERE!

SOPHIE!

HEY, CUZ. THANKS FOR COMING TO MEET ME.

LET ME TAKE YOUR BAG. YOU MUST BE EXHAUSTED!

I CAN'T WAIT TO SHOW YOU AROUND *CERN*. IT'S *AMAZEBALLS!*

THAT'S WHAT MY PHYSICS TEACHER SAID.

THERE'S THIS COMIC CONTEST IN SAN DIEGO NEXT YEAR, AND I WANT TO WIN IT SO BAD.

I NEED A SUPERHERO WITH A REALLY AWESOME POWER, THOUGH-- SOMETHING THAT NO ONE HAS EVER THOUGHT OF BEFORE.

D-E-M-O-C-R-I-T-U-S.

YOU KNOW THE GREEK ALPHABET?

I LEARNED A LITTLE IN A SUMMER CLASS ON ANCIENT ART.

DEMOCRITUS WAS A COOL GUY. THE OTHER ANCIENT GREEKS SAID THAT THE UNIVERSE WAS MADE OF FOUR BUILDING BLOCKS: *EARTH, AIR, FIRE,* AND *WATER.*

BUT DEMOCRITUS SAID THAT THE UNIVERSE WAS MADE OF TINY OBJECTS THAT COULD NOT BE DIVIDED.

A-T-O-M-O-S.

DEMOCRITUS SAID...

BY CONVENTION THERE IS COLOR, BY CONVENTION SWEETNESS, BY CONVENTION BITTERNESS, BUT IN REALITY THERE ARE ATOMS AND SPACE.

HE WAS DEFINITELY ON THE RIGHT TRACK. BUT--

--OH, HERE HE IS-- J.J. THOMSON!

IN 1897, J.J. THOMSON FOUND A PARTICLE EVEN SMALLER THAN THE ATOM.

I WAS STUDYING THE NATURE OF ELECTRICITY WHEN I DETERMINED THERE MUST BE A NEGATIVELY CHARGED PARTICLE SMALLER THAN THE ATOM.

I IMAGINED THAT THE ATOM WAS A BALL OF POSITIVELY CHARGED MATTER WITH NEGATIVELY CHARGED ELECTRONS SCATTERED THROUGH-OUT...

...RATHER LIKE RAISINS IN A PLUM PUDDING.

OH, IT *IS!*

PLUM PUDDING? SOUNDS DELICIOUS!

BUT IN THE YEARS THAT FOLLOWED, SCIENTISTS FOUND THAT ATOMS AREN'T SQUISHY PLUM PUDDINGS AT ALL! THEY HAVE A DENSE *NUCLEUS* AT THE CENTER, CONTAINING *PROTONS* (WHICH HAVE A POSITIVE CHARGE) AND *NEUTRONS* (WHICH HAVE NO CHARGE).*

A CLOUD OF NEGATIVELY CHARGED *ELECTRONS* SURROUNDS THIS POSITIVELY CHARGED NUCLEUS.

THESE DAYS, SCIENTISTS KNOW THAT PROTONS AND NEUTRONS ARE MADE OF PARTICLES CALLED...

...QUARKS.

12   *THE HYDROGEN ATOM IS THE EXCEPTION. IT CONTAINS JUST ONE PROTON AND ONE ELECTRON.

15

16

SO THAT'S ALL THERE IS TO THE STANDARD MODEL-- SIX QUARKS?

NOPE! THE MODEL ALSO INCLUDES *LEPTONS*--SIX OF THEM. REMEMBER HOW QUARKS ALWAYS HANG OUT IN GROUPS? LEPTONS ARE THE OPPOSITE-- THEY'RE LONERS.

LET'S SEE IF I CAN FIND--

AH! GOT ONE!

HERE'S A LEPTON YOU KNOW: THE *ELECTRON!*

LEMME TRY.

I THINK I SEE ANOTHER LEPTON.

KINDA HEAVY.

THAT'S A *MUON*-- KIND OF LIKE THE ELECTRON'S COUSIN.

LIKE THE ELECTRON, IT'S ALSO NEGATIVELY CHARGED, BUT THE MUON'S ABOUT 200 TIMES AS MASSIVE.

OH, LOOK!

THIS ONE'S -URK- THE *TAU* LEPTON. IT'S MORE THAN 3,000 TIMES AS MASSIVE AS THE ELECTRON.

I WOULDN'T WANT TO GET WOMPED BY ONE OF THOSE.

DON'T WORRY. THE MUON AND THE TAU LEPTONS AREN'T STABLE--

19

QUARKS

UP · DOWN · STRANGE · CHARM · BOTTOM · TOP

LEPTONS

ELECTRON · MUON · TAU · ELECTRON NEUTRINO · MUON NEUTRINO · TAU NEUTRINO

BOSONS

PHOTON · GLUON · W · Z

OKAY. SO-- SIX QUARKS, SIX LEPTONS, AND FOUR (MAYBE FIVE) BOSONS... IS THAT IT?

AHEM, NOT QUITE.

IT'S PETER HIGGS!

THE STANDARD MODEL WAS A GOOD THEORY, BUT IT HAD ONE RATHER SERIOUS PROBLEM--

IT COULDN'T EXPLAIN WHY SOME PARTICLES HAVE MASS.

UH-OH.

PETER HIGGS...

...AS IN "THE HIGGS BOSON"!

IN 1964, SOME COLLEAGUES* AND I PROPOSED THAT THERE MUST BE A FIELD AND A BOSON RATHER LIKE THE ELECTROMAGNETIC FIELD WITH ITS PHOTON BUT DIFFERENT.

FUNDAMENTAL PARTICLES GAIN MASS AS THEY INTERACT WITH THIS OTHER FIELD. THE MORE THEY INTERACT WITH THE FIELD, THE MORE MASS THEY HAVE--

HIGGS BOSON

AND THIS BOSON IS ITS FORCE CARRIER.

*FRANÇOIS ENGLERT, ROBERT BROUT, GERALD GURALNIK, CARL HAGEN, AND TOM KIBBLE.

...FOR A **COLLISION** IN A SPECIALLY DESIGNED DETECTOR.

FOLLOW US. WE'LL SHOW YOU THE ONE WE WORK ON--IT'S PART OF THE *ATLAS* EXPERIMENT.

AFTER A SHORT WALK...

THIS IS THE *ATLAS* DETECTOR!

THERE'S ANOTHER DETECTOR ON THE OTHER SIDE OF THE RING. THAT ONE BELONGS TO THE *CMS EXPERIMENT.* THE TWO DETECTORS HAVE DIFFERENT DESIGNS, WITH THEIR OWN STRENGTHS AND WEAKNESSES.

AND DIFFERENT TEAMS OF SCIENTISTS RUN EACH ONE. THAT WAY, WE CAN CONFIRM EACH OTHER'S RESULTS.

WOW! IT'S *HUGE!* CAN WE LOOK INSIDE?

MUON SPECTROMETER

MUON SPECTROMETER

MUON SPECTROMETER

MOST OF THE PARTICLES MADE BY THE COLLISION STOP IN THE CALORIMETER, EXCEPT FOR *NEUTRINOS*--WHICH GO RIGHT ON THEIR MERRY WAY, BECAUSE THEY RARELY REACT WITH ANYTHING--

WHY IS THIS TRACK *CURVED?*

HADRONIC CALORIMETER

MUON

--AND THE *MUONS.* WE ONLY DETECT THEM AS THEY PASS THROUGH THE OUTERMOST CHAMBER.

GOOD OBSERVATION, DETECTIVE!

NEUTRINO

ELECTROMAGNETIC CALORIMETER

PHOTON

PROTON

NEUTRON

PARTICLES WITH POSITIVE AND NEGATIVE CHARGES CURVE IN OPPOSITE DIRECTIONS IN A MAGNETIC FIELD. SO WE KNOW THAT THIS TRACK WAS MADE BY A POSITIVELY CHARGED PARTICLE.

TRACKING CHAMBER

MUONS-- THOSE ARE LIKE THE ELECTRON'S MORE MASSIVE COUSINS.

SPEEDY PARTICLES DON'T BEND MUCH, SINCE THEY ZIP THROUGH THE MAGNETIC FIELD SO QUICKLY. *SLOWER* PARTICLES LEAVE MORE OF A CURVED PATH.

WE CAN SEE *HOW FAST* THE PARTICLE IS MOVING TOO--ANOTHER CLUE TO ITS *IDENTITY!*

AFTER YEARS OF HARD WORK, SCIENTISTS AT DIFFERENT LABS WERE FINALLY ABLE TO I.D. EVERY ONE OF THE PARTICLES PREDICTED BY THE STANDARD MODEL...

...EXCEPT FOR THE *HIGGS BOSON!*

51

THESE LINES SHOW TRACES OF THE ELECTRON AND POSITRON, AND TRACK THE ESCAPE OF A MUON AND AN ANTIMUON.

AFTER MONTHS OF ANALYSIS, THE ATLAS AND CMS EXPERIMENTS WERE BOTH PRETTY SURE THAT THEY HAD *FINALLY FOUND* THE HIGGS BOSON.

AND SO WE GOT READY TO *REVEAL OUR RESULTS TO THE WORLD!*

I REMEMBER I WAS *SO* EXCITED WHEN MOM AND DAD GOT ME INTO THE AUDITORIUM FOR THE *BIG ANNOUNCE-MENT!*

JULY 4, 2012. GENEVA, SWITZERLAND.

JOE INCANDELA
SPOKESPERSON FOR THE CMS EXPERIMENT

FABIOLA GIANOTTI
SPOKESPERSON FOR THE ATLAS EXPERIMENT

ROLF HEUER
DIRECTOR-GENERAL OF CERN

WE OBSERVE IN OUR DATA CLEAR SIGNS OF A NEW PARTICLE, AT THE LEVEL OF *FIVE SIGMA**.

THANKS, NATURE!

AS A LAYMAN I WOULD NOW SAY, I THINK *WE HAVE IT.* DO YOU AGREE? WE HAVE REACHED A MILESTONE IN OUR UNDERSTANDING OF NATURE.

THIS IS A VERY, VERY PRELIMINARY RESULT, BUT WE THINK IT'S *STRONG.*

FIVE SIGMA-- THAT MEANS THAT THEY'RE **99.9999% **SURE** OF THEIR RESULT.*

THIS MAKES ALL OF THE LATE NIGHTS AT THE LAB WORTHWHILE!

CLAP! CLAP!

PETER HIGGS
BRITISH PHYSICIST

FOR ME, IT'S REALLY AN INCREDIBLE THING THAT IT'S HAPPENED IN MY LIFETIME.

CLAP! HOORAY! CLAP! CLAP! HOORAY! CLAP! CLAP!

CLAP! HOORAY! CLAP! CLAP! CLAP!

THAT DAY WAS TRULY AN OCCASION TO CELEBRATE!

I THINK *WE* SHOULD CELEBRATE WITH SOME ICE CREAM AT THE CAFETERIA.

EXCELLENT IDEA!

YEAH!

LATER...

IT'S KIND OF SAD, ISN'T IT?

SAD? WHY DO YOU SAY THAT?

NOW THAT THEY'VE FOUND THE HIGGS BOSON, THERE'S *NOTHING LEFT* TO FIND.

OH, THERE ARE *LOTS* OF UNANSWERED QUESTIONS!

LIKE WHY DO WE GET *ZITS* AT THE WORST POSSIBLE TIME?

I GUESS YOU'D HAVE TO ASK THE BIOLOGISTS ABOUT *THAT*. BUT THERE ARE COUNTLESS PHYSICS MYSTERIES. LIKE THE LITTLE PROBLEM OF *DARK MATTER*.

WHATEVER *THAT* IS!

AND WE *DON'T* KNOW WHAT IT IS!

SO--YOU'RE TELLING ME THAT YOU'RE LOOKING FOR SOMETHING THAT YOU *CAN'T FIND*, BUT YOU DON'T KNOW WHAT YOU'RE *LOOKING FOR*.

EXACTLY!

AND WHAT'S REALLY INCREDIBLE IS ALL THE STUFF WE CAN DETECT--STARS, PLANETS, THE WHOLE SHEBANG--ACCOUNTS FOR *ONLY 4%* OF THE UNIVERSE!

SO...MOST OF THE UNIVERSE IS *INVISIBLE?*

YEAH! WE THINK THAT ABOUT *ONE-QUARTER OF THE UNIVERSE* IS ACTUALLY *MADE* OF DARK MATTER.

WHAT IS IT?!

WE DON'T KNOW! BUT WE HAVE SOME THEORIES. IT MAY BE A *KIND OF PARTICLE* MADE AFTER THE BIG BANG.

WHAT'S EVEN STRANGER IS THAT REGULAR MATTER AND DARK MATTER TOGETHER ONLY ACCOUNT FOR ABOUT *A THIRD* OF THE UNIVERSE.

OBSERVABLE MATTER AND ENERGY

DARK MATTER

YOU'RE *FREAKIN' ME OUT!*

THE REST? A MYSTERIOUS FORM OF ENERGY-- *DARK ENERGY*-- THAT SEEMS TO BE EMBEDDED IN THE FABRIC OF SPACE AND TIME.

DARK ENERGY

THE UNIVERSE IS EXPANDING FASTER AND FASTER. AND WE BELIEVE *DARK ENERGY* COUNTERACTS GRAVITY'S TENDENCY TO SLOW THE EXPANSION DOWN.

BUT WHAT DOES *THAT* MEAN...?

OH! I GET IT--THERE *HAS* TO BE ENERGY INVOLVED, BECAUSE OF THE "E" IN $E=MC^2$!

YEP.

Unsolved Mysteries of Particle Physics

Dark matter and dark energy are among the most important unsolved mysteries in physics. But physicists will be examining other unanswered questions for years to come.

Why Is the Universe Made of Matter and Not Antimatter?

All known matter particles have corresponding antimatter particles, with the same mass but opposite electric charges. As soon as antimatter comes into contact with matter, it disappears in a flash of energy. (Scientists have learned this through making antimatter in colliders.) Since scientists theorize that the big bang should have created equal amounts of matter and antimatter, people wonder: Why didn't matter and antimatter cancel each other out at the very beginning? Somehow—no one is quite sure *how*—a tiny bit of matter gained an edge on antimatter. It's possible that matter won out because antimatter particles decay at a faster rate than matter particles. In fact, scientists are testing that hypothesis at the Large Hadron Collider!

Why Is Gravity So Weak Compared with the Other Fundamental Forces?

One theory says that gravity seems so weak relative to the other forces because people just don't feel its full force. According to this theory, part of gravity spreads to other dimensions. Humans live their everyday lives in three spatial dimensions (and in time, the fourth dimension). But additional, hidden dimensions may exist on a very small scale. Picture an acrobat walking a tightrope. The acrobat can move backward or forward, but not left, right, up, or down. But an ant walking along that tightrope can also travel *around* the rope. The ant lives on a smaller scale, and its world includes that extra dimension.

If gravity carrier particles (gravitons) exist, scientists might be able to make them at the European Organization for Nuclear Research. But the particles would immediately disappear into that extra dimension. The scientists, operating within our three-dimensional world, would only see that a piece of the puzzle was missing. However, if they were able to look at the rest of the puzzle—the other products of a collision—they would see some missing energy that might reveal more about the graviton.

Is It Worth It?

Particle physics research isn't cheap. Construction of the Large Hadron Collider required about $4.75 billion. Use of the collider requires an additional $1 billion every year. The money comes from the governments and institutions of participating countries. While many of the physicists at the LHC are simply interested in learning more about how the universe works, society often reaps the benefits of research in surprising ways.

Because physicists are always pushing the limits of science, they often have to build their own instruments. And many of the ideas that went into building these new machines—not to mention the technology itself—are useful to the rest of the world. We wouldn't have computers, X-rays, or global positioning systems without fundamental science research. Magnetic resonance imaging (MRI)—a powerful medical diagnostic tool—uses a magnetic field and radio waves to look inside the body. It uses superconducting magnets, the same kind used at the LHC. These kinds of magnets were first built for a particle accelerator in the United States. The touch screen technology in tablets and smartphones was also developed at CERN. And a computer scientist at CERN who wanted to find a way for scientists around the world to share information invented the World Wide Web. Would you say it's worth the price tag?

Science on the Move

Scientific advances can develop quickly! In fact, as this book was going to publication, new data from the LHC indicated that scientists may have detected yet another new particle. It may come to nothing, or it could be an exciting game changer that will shake our understanding of the Standard Model. By the time you read this, we'll probably know.

Peter Higgs

Transforming the Standard Model

Peter Higgs has always been something of an outsider. He was born in the northeastern corner of England in 1929, but his family moved from place to place, following his father's job as a sound engineer with the British Broadcasting Corporation. Higgs also had severe asthma—and in the days before effective drugs, this was a really big deal. As a result of his family's frequent moves and his illness, Higgs missed a lot of school. His mother often taught him at home.

At the age of twelve, Higgs enrolled in a grammar school in Bristol, England. World War II was raging during this time, and Bristol took heavy bombing. Shortly after arriving at his new school, Higgs fell into a crater in the playground—a crater left by a German bomb. Later, the Higgs family had to move after unexploded bombs were found across the road from their home. These events led Higgs to protest against the atomic bomb as a teenager. By this time, he had become interested in science, but unlike many physicists of the day, he wanted nothing to do with warfare.

Higgs's eyes would often wander during secondary school assemblies. More than once, he noticed a board listing his school's most honored alumni. One name appeared several times: Paul Dirac. Higgs did a little research on this Nobel Prize–winning alumni and found that Dirac was the father of quantum mechanics—the laws of physics that apply to subatomic particles. This kind of science, Higgs thought, could explain the way the world worked.

Higgs proceeded to study physics at a London college. After a series of failed experiments, he concluded that he was not cut out to work in a lab. He was better off using his brain to develop theories that others could test. At the age of twenty-one, Higgs gave a speech to a scientific society at the college. His theme—*How can scientists be sure that the observations they make are real?*—would be answered sixty-two years later by a $10 billion collider.

In 1960, Higgs took a position at a university in Edinburgh, Scotland. He became interested in the question of why particles gain mass. Skepticism surrounded the main theory of the time, but no one could figure out a better theory. Most people thought this field of research was a dead end. Higgs, ever the outsider, kept plugging away at it. One day in the summer of 1964, he had an "aha!" moment after reading a new research paper by a colleague. He spent the weekend walking the hills around Edinburgh and thinking. The paper he wrote afterward described a new type of field that would give particles mass via a carrier boson. It was published (after being rejected by an editor from CERN) in September 1964.

François Englert

Particle Physics Pioneer

François Englert *(top right)* was seven years old in 1940, the year the Nazis invaded his home country of Belgium. Englert and his family were forced to wear yellow Star of David patches identifying them as Jewish. As the Nazis began to send other Belgian Jews to concentration camps, François's family sent him to live with a Christian couple in a small Belgian village, while his parents and brother took refuge elsewhere. The Englerts hoped that splitting up their family might increase their chances of survival. Later, when the family reunited in another small village, a priest told village residents that the newcomers were Christian. He also baptized François so that François could attend a Catholic school.

The Englert family survived the Holocaust, although many of the Englerts' relatives did not. After the war, François developed a love for mathematics, music, and literature. However, his parents wanted him to study something practical, so like a good son, he earned a degree in electrical and mechanical engineering. His heart wasn't in it, though—Englert was more interested in learning the secrets of the universe than in building things. And so he went back to school. By 1959, he had earned his doctorate in physics.

Degree in hand, Englert accepted an offer to work for two years with Robert Brout *(top left, page 66)*, a young professor in New York. Englert returned to Belgium in 1961, but he soon missed collaborating with Brout. Brout missed working with Englert too. Brout and his wife moved to Belgium the same year.

Englert and Brout wanted to understand more about the first moments following the big bang. The two physicists proposed that immediately after this moment, particles had no mass. But as the universe expanded and cooled, a kind of phase transition took place, as when water turns to ice. An invisible field grew out of that phase transition, and any particle that interacted with that field gained mass. Englert and Brout published their findings in August 1964.

Both François Englert and Peter Higgs continued their exploration of particle physics in the decades that followed. In 2013, the Royal Swedish Academy of Sciences awarded Englert and Higgs the Nobel Prize in Physics for their theory explaining why particles have mass. Robert Brout passed away in 2011, before the discovery of the Higgs boson. Otherwise, Brout surely would have joined Englert and Higgs on the Nobel Prize stage in 2013. Three other physicists, Tom Kibble, Gerald Guralnik, and Carl Hagen *(left to right, page 66)*, published a paper describing a similar theory of particles and mass in November 1964. Although these physicists surely deserve credit for their groundbreaking work, the Royal Swedish Academy of Sciences awards the Nobel Prize to no more than three people at a time.

Glossary

accelerator: a machine that brings particles to very high speeds

annihilation: the process that occurs when a particle collides with its antiparticle, resulting in their transformation into new particles

antimatter particles: particles that are identical in all respects to their matter partners except for an opposite charge

beam: in physics, the stream of particles injected into an accelerator

big bang theory: the scientific theory that all space, time, matter, and energy originated from the violent expansion of a singular point of extremely high density and temperature

boson: a class of particles including the force-carrying particles (photons, gluons, and W and Z bosons), the Higgs boson, and the graviton

CERN: the European Organization for Nuclear Research, an accelerator laboratory near Geneva, Switzerland

collider: an accelerator in which two beams of particles make contact

dark energy: a difficult-to-detect form of energy that may accelerate the expansion of the universe

dark matter: matter that exists in the universe but that humans cannot detect because it emits no radiation that humans can observe

decay: the process in which a single particle transforms into multiple lighter particles

electromagnetic force: the physical interaction between electrically charged particles. It is one of the four fundamental forces.

electron: a lepton and, along with protons and neutrons, a building block of atoms. The electron is the least massive lepton. It carries an electric charge of -1.

event: in physics, the collision of two particles or the decay of a single particle

flavor: in physics, the term used to organize the different types of quarks and leptons

gluon: the carrier particle of the strong force

gravitational force: the force of attraction between all masses in the universe. It is the weakest of the four fundamental forces.

graviton: the theoretical carrier particle of the gravitational force

hadron: a particle made of quarks or antiquarks or both

Higgs boson: the carrier particle of the Higgs field, which is believed to give particles mass

lepton: a class of fundamental particle that does not interact strongly with other particles

LHC: the Large Hadron Collider at the CERN laboratory. The LHC is the most powerful particle accelerator in the world.

mass: the energy of a particle at rest, divided by the speed of light squared

muon: the second-heaviest lepton, with a charge of -1

neutrino: a lepton with no electrical charge and very little mass. Neutrinos participate only in weak and gravitational interactions and are very difficult to detect.

neutron: along with the proton and electron, one of the building blocks of the atom. Neutrons have no electric charge and are made of two down quarks and an up quark.

nucleus: in physics, the dense region of protons and neutrons at the center of an atom

photon: the force carrier particle of the electromagnetic force

proton: along with the neutron and the electron, one of the building blocks of the atom. Protons have a positive electric charge and are made of two up quarks and a down quark.

quark: one of the fundamental particles of matter. Quarks come in six flavors: up, down, strange, charm, bottom, and top. Only the up and down quarks are commonly found in nature.

standard model: a theory of fundamental particles and interactions

strong force: one of four fundamental forces. This force brings quarks together to make hadrons and holds protons and neutrons together in atomic nuclei.

tau lepton: the heaviest lepton, with a charge of -1

W boson: a carrier particle of the weak force

weak force: one of the four fundamental forces. It causes the decay of massive quarks and leptons into lighter particles.

Z boson: a carrier particle of the weak force

Further Information

Books

Carroll, Sean. *The Particle at the End of the Universe: How the Hunt for the Higgs Boson Leads Us to the Edge of a New World*. New York: Plume, 2013. For older readers.

Gilliland, Ben. *Rocket Science for the Rest of Us: Cutting-Edge Concepts Made Simple*. New York: DK, 2015.

Marisco, Katie. *Key Discoveries in Physical Science*. Minneapolis: Lerner Publications, 2015.

Randall, Lisa. *Higgs Discovery: The Power of Empty Space*. New York: Ecco Solo, 2013. For older readers.

Visual Media

Cosmos: A Spacetime Odyssey. First broadcast in 2014 by Fox. Directed by Brannon Braga, Ann Druyan, and Bill Pope. Written by Ann Druyan and Steven Soter. Produced by Cosmos Studios, Fuzzy Door Productions, and Santa Fe Studios, 2014. In this documentary series, scientist and host Neil deGrasse Tyson explores how humans discovered the laws of nature and found our coordinates in space and time.

Particle Fever. Directed by Mark Levinson. Produced by Mark Levinson and David Kaplan, 2013. This documentary film provides a close look at the search for—and discovery of—the Higgs boson.

Websites

ATLAS Experiment
http://www.atlas.ch

CERN: Accelerating Science
http://home.web.cern.ch

CMS (Compact Muon Solenoid) Experiment
http://cms.web.cern.ch

The Particle Adventure: Fundamentals of Matter and Force
http://www.particleadventure.org/index.html

About the Author

Sara Latta began writing about science and medicine after receiving a master's degree in immunology. Later, she earned a master of fine arts in creative writing from Lesley University in Cambridge, MA. She lives in New York City with her husband, a physicist and dean of sciences at City College of New York, and their children. Latta is a member of the Society of Children's Book Writers and Illustrators, the National Association of Science Writers, and the Authors Guild. Visit her at www.saralatta.com.

About the Illustrator

Jeff Weigel is an illustrator, author, and designer of children's books and graphic novels. Weigel illustrated the 2009 *New York Times* best seller *It's Beginning to Look a Lot Like Zombies: A Book of Zombie Christmas Carols*, and he wrote, illustrated, and designed *Stop Math*, an interactive tablet storybook. He was also a regular contributor to Image Comics' anthology title, *Big Bang Comics*, for more than 10 years. His latest book is the middle-grade graphic novel *Dragon Girl: The Secret Valley*. He has served as a graphic designer and commercial illustrator for many years as well. Find out more at www.jeffweigel.com.